Splash!

A waterpark mystery

this page intensionally left blank

BATHTUB

SPLASH

A waterpark mystery

MOORE-FUN

Now with skill builder practice and a book quiz!

www.YMBAgroup.com

Dedicated to children and siblings.
Thank you for the fun!

The characters and events in this story are not real. Locations, events, ideas and characters in this story are intended to be fictional.

Note that permission is not granted by the author for any part of this publication to be copied, recorded, photographed or stored in any type of retrieval or download system, or in any similar style for manner as indicated above. To request permission for any part of this book, or any other book by the author, visit: www.ymbagroup.com.

ISBN: 1986316041
ISBN 13: 978-1986316040

Createspace Publishing, 2018

Printed in the U.S.A.

Contact: www.YMBAgroup.com

Chapter 1

Morgan stands by the big, front window moving her head left and right as her hair shifts side to side. Morgan is watching a man get out of a green pick-up truck.

Morgan is worried. She looks toward the animals outside in the pen and whispers, "Oh no, I don't think our pigs will like him."

Zack overhears and with super fast nine-year-old speed he goes to Morgan at the window. He can't wait to look outside with his seven-year-old sister. This is the first chance to see the man who will take care of his pigs.

In a loud voice Zack questions to his mother in

the next room, "That's the man who will take care of my prize pigs while we're away? You are right Morgan. Hazel the pig is sure to run away!" Mom walks across the family room and softly readjusts the curtains so the children are no longer able to see outside.

"Ok children, now let us get back to packing. Zack, Hazel the pig is beautiful like hazel eyes. Farmer Hammond will care for her. Hazel will be fine while we travel on our family adventure. Please go to your room to finish packing for our trip. Keep your ears open. Father will call to leave in just a few minutes."

Mom looks to the kitchen and calls to her husband, "Tom, Farmer Hammond is here."

"Morgan, follow me." Zack instructs his younger sister.

Zack runs up the stairs with his backpack on his shoulder. The brother and sister zoom past their twin sisters bedroom. Inside the twin girls have a bedroom filled with the colors of pink and purple. The twins Rachel and Reese are in the room talking about what to pack for the family RV road trip .

Eleven-year-old Reese tells her sister her problem.

"Rachel, one year of outfits to plan! I can't decide what to wear tomorrow!"

Rachel is clearly distracted by the messy suitcase Reese has on her bed. Rachel listens to her sister while she takes balls of clothes out of Reese's bag. Rachel likes neat and tiny packing. Reese is too busy trying to make outfits to pack neatly. Rachel helps her sister by foling the clothes neatly in the suitcase.

As Rachel is folding her sisters clothes she replies, "Reese, whatever you bring is fine. I've never seen someone pack for days and still not be ready. You began packing last week! If only you could pack your shirts as fast as your artist pencils and science kit we would be on the road!"

Reese lets out a sigh and plops down on her bed. "Oh Rachel, I just don't know what I want to wear next week. What is the weather? Where will we be? How will I be ready to leave on time?

Rachel moves over to sit close to her sister and says, "Reese, a one year RV tour with our family is fun, in any outfit you wear. You can do this, ok?

Let's be excited for our adventure. If you want to be ready when dad calls then now is the time to stop worrying. Let's go Reese -pack, pack, pack!" Reese takes a deep breath. Reese stands up from her pink bed and ties back her long brown hair into a high ponytail.

"You are right Rachel. I'll be down stairs in ten minutes. Tell dad not to leave without me." Rachel nods and says, "Will do!".

Rachel walks over to her purple bed to pick up her two bags. Rachel lets out a groan as she lifts and mumbles, "Whew! Books are heavy! Where is our brother Battle when I need him?"

Reese quickly answers, "At least you are packed! My style ideas just clicked and mom and dad are going to call for us to leave any minute. I have to work fast and fill my bag!"

Fifteen minutes later

"Maggie, Battle, Reese, Rachel, Zack, Morgan - say good-bye to the farm, its time to get on board our happy RV!"

Reese is still packing as the loud bellow rings through the house. It is their dad. His voice has a

8

way of reaching each room in the farmhouse and sound as if he is standing right there. Each member of the family heard dad.

The first voice to answer is the oldest child in the family, Battle.

"Coming dad! Mom - I'm going to the RV." Battle hollers his answer from his bedroom. Battle puts on his Tennessee Tigers baseball cap. The cap covers his blonde hair that happens to be the same exact hair color as Morgan's. The Tigers are a local minor league baseball team. Battle hopes to one day hear the town cheer him on as a player at one of the games. Battle is ready to go and walking down the stairs with a slow strut and the usual sports bag slung over his shoulder, he is the first to exit the house to meet dad at the RV.

A second sound makes its way around the house. *kuhplunk, boom, boom*

"Reese is that you? Are you ok?" Mom asks over the sound of Zack's laughter.

"Yes, mom. I just dropped my things on the stairs." Reese gathers her things and continues out the front door to the RV.

Zack looks up at his mother, "Mom, don't worry. It would not be a 'real day' if Reese did not bump into something, drop something or fall down."

In a loud voice from the living room Rachel calls to her mom who is standing at the front door. "Mom, I'm just finishing this chapter so I can have one less book to carry in my bag. I will be there in five minutes."

Mom quickly answers.

"Rachel, it's time to go. Your dad is waiting at the RV. You can bring your book or finish it next year when we get back. Please help Morgan with her bags."

Rachel answers her mother, "Ok, will do mom. Morgan and I are on our way."

Zack taps and tugs his mom on the arm and in a whiny, but sweet, voice asks, "Mom, can I go to the RV now? I have to be in the RV before Morgan or she'll take the good seat!"

Mom gives permission.

"Zack, you may go outside and meet dad and your brother Battle. Carry your own bag out of the house please. Go directly to the RV, no pig visits please."

Before leaving Zack tries once again for a hint on where they are going.

Zack taps his mother on her arm, "Mom, between you and me. Where is our first stop on the trip?" Mom smirks and gives Zack a hug with a smile.

"Zack, I can always count on you to try one more time. Sorry, no hints. Try to enjoy the drive and we will be there soon."

Zack shrugs, "Let's get to it then!" and runs out the front door to go to the RV.

Rachel, Morgan and mom are the last family members in the house. Mom does one last walk to check the house to make sure all the packed bags made it to the RV.

Showing a big smile mom says, "Rachel, Morgan, it looks like we are ready to go. Let's make our way to your father and begin our family adventure!"

Chapter 2

The RV is filled with happy energy as the Moore family prepares to start the trip. Once everyone is inside the RV the children begin to choose their sleeping spaces. Rachel and Reese make a quick claim on the bunk beds, but that is ok with everyone else. The bunk bed area is narrow so that even turning over requires someone to flip with care. Battle and Zack both choose the bed above the driver called the "second floor". Mom and Morgan will sleep in the back of the RV. Morgan proudly says it is her first bedroom to have a television and a view. Dad has a bedroom that is less permanent. At the end of the day, and since he is the last one awake, dad will convert the dining area to his sleeping space. So dad will be sleeping on a table!

After five minutes Dad says loudly, "Moore family … time to take your seats".

Zack goes to his seat and opens the window closest to his seatin the RV. Zack opens his window and stands on his knees on the seat. He waves his hand outside and looks for a moment to look for Farmer Hammond.

"Take care of my pigs – they are prize swine you know - and they like corn!"

Zack then closes the window, sits down in his seat. Zack looks around the RV. Talking to himself Zack says,

"I am not sure about this day. An old farmer is in charge of my pigs and my little sister is in the good seat."

Hearing her brother Morgan answers with the sweetest smile.

"Zack, I cannot help it if you were too busy making your bed to hold your own seat. You know mom's rule. Any open seat is for 'anyone'. I am an 'anyone' and you were too late!"

Dad turns to look back from the driver seat. Saying the words he is sure to speak 300 more times,

"Buckle up Moore Family for moorrreee safety."

Next is the seatbelt check for all on *The Happy RV*. After the last "check" is said in the RV dad knows all seven seatbelts are clicked in. The RV goes from park to drive.

The last year has been full of planning for and thinking about the trip. The next year is sure to be full of excitement!

The family road trip begins!

Chapter 3

A few hours go by as the family settles into the RV.

Zack leans forward in his seat toward his mother and asks,

"Mom, how much longer?"

"Zack, it has only been two hours!"

Rachel quickly answers from her seat behind him.

Zack turns to look at his sister.

"Rachel, you're not mom."

Zack turns to look at mom and leans forward to whisper.

"Mom, can we at least have a clue? How much longer? I won't say word."

Mom answers with a grin and speaks loud so

everyone in the RV can hear her.

"Sorry kids. You each know my rule. Sit back and enjoy the ride. Dad and I planned the trip and want to surprise you with each of the 'family fun stops.'"

"Daaaad ..", Zack nags.

Dad shakes his head and smiles at Zack.

"Zack, you know I am not the one with the plans. I am the family driver, Sir. Your mom has the plan book."

Zack is not ready to stop talking. Zack looks at mom and tries again.

"Mom, can you tell me when we will be there? Even if you don't want to tell me where *there* is going to be. Can I have even a little clue?"

Reese joins in by speaking loudly from her seat in the back of the RV.

Reese asks, "Mom please give him the clue so he will stop asking! I was drawing a happy picture, but now my characters are starting to look less than happy."

"We can't have that can we Reese. Ok, kids, here is a little bitty detail of the plan. We will stop at a campground tonight to sleep. We will be at the campground in about three hours. Then, after we wake up tomorrow, we have a one hour drive to our first 'family fun stop'!"

The five children cheer with joy. The RV fills with the sound of the kids talking to each other. Rachel checks the map to try to guess where the family will go the next day.

A few minutes later the sound of AM radio comes from each speaker in the RV. Listening to talking on AM radio is Dad's favorite; not music. The radio loud and its words fill can not be ignored in the RV. The kids one at a time with a moan or a groan place their headphones on their head. The AM radio is not their favorite.

Quickly the RV is quiet as the kids read, color and listen to music with their headphones.

Dad enjoys the quiet drive listening to his fuzzy stations on the radio.

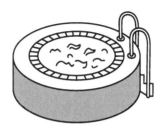

Chapter 4

Beep Beep Beep Beep ...

Early the next morning the alarm clock rings at seven o'clock at the camp ground. Battle, Rachel, Reese, Zack and Morgan each hurry out of bed. The kids are excited to learn their surprise 'family fun stop' for the day.

The first three minutes of the day were quiet. The kids were awake, but quiet. Then at 7:04 am Morgan says the first words of the day.

"Mom, are you ready? Mom, can I talk to you? What are we doing today?"

Morgan asks all three questions as if they are one big sentence. Each question is asked with a look

18

of hope that mom will give a clue.

Mom sits up in bed and looks at Morgan.

In a fun way Mom moves her head from right to left to say no to Morgan. Mom answers her with words so all in the RV can hear.

"Morgan, you kids are not ready at all. You have to get ready."

A look of surprise travels from Battle to Rachel to Reese to Zack to Morgan. Then each of the five children look to mom.

Mom laughs and looks at dad. Mom gives dad a wink with her eye to let dad know it is ok to reveal the 'family fun stop'.

Dad starts to guess with a big smile.

"Humm … mom, do you think it is a bathing suit day? Maybe the kids did not pack their suits?"

The RV shakes as the kids jump and cheer! The five kids dash to search their suitcases for their bathing suits.

"Battle, please play in the water with me!"

"Reese – you don't even know where we will be! But, if there is a pool I will totally do that with you!" Battle promises.

"Mom, is it a waterpark? I am not saying tell me. But, if it is we can do the lazy river. Remember, like we did at the last waterpark?" Rachel smiles.

Dad stands up. Dad points with his fingers at Morgan and Zack.

"Morgan and Zack, are you up for another ice cream contest?"

Dad smiles and rubs his stomach with his left hand while making a circle.

"Yum, yum! You both have not come close in the speed ice cream eating contest! You know how much I love you. I am giving you another chance to win."

Morgan quickly jumps up rubbing her tummy in a circle just like dad.

"Yum, yum, yum dad .. count me in!"

The children continue to move around the RV in search of their bathing suits.

Next, they begin taking turns in the bathroom to put them on.

Over the happy laughter dad shares news with the kids.

"When you are all in your bathing suits please

sit down. After I hear seven belt clicks we will drive to our first 'family fun stop'!"

One hour later the RV turns onto a road with the name Water Way.

"Moore family, welcome to 'family fun stop' number one!" Dad announces.

Suddenly, the largest bathtub the kids ever saw was only 300 feet away! It was big. It was colorful. It was awesome!

"Ooooo"

"Ahhhh"

"Wooooo Hoooo!"

Looking out the window the kids get even more excited as the RV gets closer.

"Look! There is a duck in a huge bathtub!", said Morgan.

The RV comes to a stop and dad shifts the car to park. The kids unbuckle their belts and jump from their seats.

Battle opens the RV door.

"Helloooo waterpark! Everyone follow me. I see

the ticket booth." The family gets off the RV.

Following Battle at a fast pace the family walks through the parking lot and arrives at the ticket booth.

When they arrive there they see someone in the ticket booth. Sitting on a tall stool inside the booth is a very small woman with a big, scratchy voice.

"Welcome to The Bath Tub. You have a lovely family. How many tickets?"

Dad quickly answers, "Thank you. I have grown to like them myself. Seven please" promptly answers dad as he places a credit card on the counter.

The park worker hands the tickets out the window to dad.

"Thank you for visiting. Be sure to check out the annual drain pipe race tomorrow morning at ten." Rachel elbows Battle on his side and points.

"Battle, look over there at the poster. I just read about the pipe race. You are old enough to sign up and there's a great prize!"

"What's the prize Rachel, a bookmark?" Battle jokes and continues.

"For real Rachel, what's the prize?"

"It's one-hundred bathtub bucks to use here at *The Bath Tub*. Besides, you can skip the line! Come on, you can try the tallest tube ride in the park!"

"That sounds like a great plan. I sure would not mind a *Bath Tub* baseball cap."

Battle turns to his parents.

"Mom, Dad, can I sign up for the race?"

Mom answers Battle with a thumbs-up.

"Sure, we can sign up now and then go directly to the *Hair Clog*. I see the wait time for the ride is only 10 minutes."

As the family is walking to the race registration table Reese talks with her mom.

"The *Hair Clog* .. really mom? That has to be the worst name for a water ride!"
Zack laughs.

"Nah, look here at the map. It is just a twirl ride Reese! We all sit in a raft and spin around and around. The only hair in your face is your own."

Reese ties her hair up in a ponytail as the family arrives at the sign-up table for the race.

"Kids, dad and I are going to the gift shop right

there. You all stay together and sign up Battle for the race, then wait for us at the seating area. We will be right back."

Battle answers, "Got it mom".

Rachel follows with, "Yes mom."

A few minutes later while still on line the kids read a poster for the event.

The poster says, "*The Current Champion*" with a picture of a 14-year-old boy.

"Hey Moore family, look at who I'm going to beat!" Battle says while being silly and flexing his arms to show his muscles.

A new voice comes from a boy behind Battle.

"Hi … Cliff is my name. Do you like my poster?"

Battle turns left and right to compare the poster and person talking. The person standing in front of him is the same person on the poster! Seeing that Battle is embarrassed, Reese steps forward and puts out her hand for a handshake.

"Hi Cliff, Reese here. I see you met my brother Battle. You have quite a winning steak. Any secrets you can share with him?"

Cliff shrugs his shoulders and answers.

"Reese, I'm the third person in my family to win. I guess I can say winning is a family secret. My brothers both won also. I was signing up here and then I'll be walking over to practice for the race. All contestants are welcome to practice. Battle, will I see you there in a few minutes?" Battle happily answers.

"You bet! See you there!"

Chapter 5

"Ooohhh Battle .. look at all those steps!"

Morgan is looking up at the tube slides for the slide race. The tubes look like three slithering snakes coming up and out of a bathtub.

Rachel looks up at the tubes.

"I don't understand why someone would walk up all those stairs just to come down one of those tubes. A slide like that is not for me – one look down and I'll puke on the people below."

Reese says, "Rachel, you haven't puked yet in the RV, maybe you lost your crown as Puke Queen."

"All I know is I'm glad my prize pigs are not here to get barfed on." Zack tells his sisters.

"But. I do think it would be fun to hear the pigs squeal on the way down".

Morgan taps Zack on his arm.

"Zack, I'm glad the pigs are not here. If a pig squeals it is not happy. I love your little piggies!"

Talking over the voices of his siblings Battle has something to say to everyone.

"As dad would say … I am going now to go get Mooorrreeee trophies!"

Battle heads to practice and the kids choose an area in the bleacher seating nearby to watch the practice slides. Also sitting in the bleacher seats are the two older brothers of Cliff. Cliff was last years champion that is on the poster for the race this year.

"Looks like there is a fan club for Cliff. Those guys must be his brothers wearing the "Team Cliff" shirts." Rachel says.

The minutes tick by, but no one has come down the tube sllides yet. Zack is very bored. He begins making paper airplanes with park maps.

Rachel looks at Zack.

"Zack, why can't you sit still for a few minutes

and wait to clap for Battle? Why are you always busy? It's too hot for airplanes anyway."

Zack shrugs his shoulders and continues to throw his airplanes.   One airplane lands close to Cliff's brothers with the matching Team Cliff shirts.

Zack looks to Reese for help.

"Zack, you have to get it."

"Reese, come on. You're my big sister, you get it."

"Sorry Zack, if you stopped when I said this ..."

"Ok, Reese. I'll get it."

With a shy look on his face Zack quietly walks toward the brothers to get his airplane.

Zack hears the brothers talking about the race.

"… it has to be slide three; just like all the other years. You told Cliff right?"

"Yes - yes, he knows, stop talking about this here."

The brothers are talking in whispers.

"I know, but he barely won last year and –"

"But, he still won, and Cliff knows about slide three, so he knows what he needs to know."

Zack stops in his footsteps.

What did he just hear? Zack decides to leave his airplane on the ground and turns to run back to his sisters, Rachel, Reese and Morgan.

Trying to catch his breath Zack begins to talk.

"We have to get to Battle and tell him the news!"

Morgan, moving her right pointer finger from left to right, answers Zack first.

"Zack, even I know Battle is busy now."

Zack with worry on his face, "I'm going, and you can come with me or not."

Reese takes Zack by the hand, "Zack, Battle will be done with practice in thirty minutes. The race is tomorrow, so we do not want him to miss any practice time. You can see him in 30 minutes. What is it you have to tell him anyway?"

Looking around to make sure no one is listening Zack leans in to talk quietly.

"Reese, Cliff has it rigged! The champion is a cheat! I think his brothers know the secret plan! Battle does not have a chance! We have to tell him what they are up to!"

Zack secretly points to the brothers.

"Don't you see Reese, they made it so the only winner of the race will be their brother Cliff!"

Rachel moves to sit close to Zack and Morgan.

"What are you talking about? What did you hear? Why are you are talking so fast!", Rachel asks.

Zack tells his sisters what he heard the brothers say when he went to get his airplane.

"I am sure the brothers have something planned with slide three. That is how they win each year."

"Zack, before we worry Battle, let us go closer to the slides and look to see if we can figure it out."

"Ok Rachel, but when we tell Battle I want him to know it was my discovery!"

Reese is excited to be able to use her camera.

"I have my camera here. I can zoom in close to see the small details." Reese says.

Reese, Rachel, Morgan and Zack spend the next 30 minutes looking at the slides. Reese is sure to take pictures of the slides from all sides.

As the kids are finishing their inspection Rachel leans close to Zach.

"Zack, wait to tell Battle what you heard until we are in the RV for lunch. That way no one will hear you. I am sure Battle will know what to do."

Zack gives Rachel a thumbs up. Morgan and Reese also give a thumbs-up to tell Battle at the RV.

Chapter 6

Rachel is tapping a pencil at the table in the RV. Mom is putting sandwiches on the table. Zack begins to talk.

"You won't believe .."

and is quickly interrupted by Rachel who finishes his sentence.

"You won't believe the big bird we saw today."

"A big bird huh?" dad answers.

"I didn't know you liked ornithology – the study of birds."

Dad is wondering what Zack wanted to say.

Reese stands up from the table.

"Not me, other animals sure, but birds - nope, I'm

31

not a bird girl like Rachel. Bu I do have something to upload on my computer."

The kids are each excited to tell their brother Battle the news about Cliff, slide number three and the race. Reese and Rachel know Battle will ask for proof. Reese works to quickly upload the pictures from her camera to the computer.

A few minutes later the pictures are on the computer. Reese works to zoom in close on the pictures to see slide three and Cliff's brothers. Reese hears the family talking as she words. Dad can be heard clearing the lunch plates from the table.

Rachel asks, "Hey, Reese – ready to bring your computer here?" Dad settles in at the sink as he cleans the dishes. The sink water is loud so dad cannot hear the children talking. Mom is in the front seat confirming the next campground reservation.

Rachel and Reese are at the table on the left side of Battle. Morgan and Zack sit on the right side of Battle.

"Um, I am as much of a family brother as anyone,

but guys .. a few inches of space?" Battle jokes.

"Battle, we have serious business. This is the real deal. We are not playing here. This is big news!"

"Ok Zack, what's up?" Battle answers.

Rachel gives Reese a nod and a nudge on her arm to tell her to start talking.

"Battle, we have some news about the race."

"Let me guess Reese, you want to tell me the winner gets bath bucks for the gift shop? Did you find a bathing suit you want?" Battle answers with a smirk on his face.

"No, well, maybe .. I don't know – but that's not what I am thinking about now. I had something to say about the race."

Zack jumps in, "I want to tell him .. I can't wait any more and I saw it first! Battle they are cheating! You don't have a chance at winning."

With his eyebrows up and eyes wide-open Battle turns to Rachel.

"Rachel, what is Zack talking about?" he asks.

"It's true Battle. As you were at practice Zack was flying paper airplanes. One landed by two people we did not know. We think they are Cliff's brothers.

Do you remember Cliff said his family had won the race before?"

Battle holds up his hand to ask Rachel to stop.

"Ya know, all because his brothers are here to cheer for him does not mean Cliff will win."

Battle begins to stand as Rachel touches his arm.

"But Battle - Zack heard the brothers talk about doing something to make sure Cliff will win."

Battle sits down and Reese starts to talk.

"Here is what we know. The brothers have an odd machine they aim at the slides. I guess it only works on slide three. They definitely want Cliff on slide three – that is for sure."

Battle is quiet. The look on his face shows that he is thinking. Then Battle remembers something.

"Come to think of it, at practice the judges said they choose the slides. But I also heard Cliff talking with a judge about seeing him at their family picnic." Battle says.

Zack jumps in with excitement.

"We have pictures Battle! We can stop them and you can still win! Show him the pictures Reese!"

"Ok, Zack. It sounds like we have to look at the

pictures to see why slide three is the one wanted by Cliff." Battle answers as he sits down again.

Reese spins her laptop toward Battle. Battle leans in close to the computer screen to look at the pictures.

"Battle, look at this. There is a camera at the bottom of each slide. The camera takes a picture at the exact second you finish the race." Rachel says.

Morgan pulls the computer to her at the table.

"I want to see also. Where's the camera?"

"Rachel, Morgan, that is not a camera, that's a laser sensor. It's how the judges know who finishes the race first. The sensor works with a beam of light. The light beam is broken when a person passes by the sensor beam of light. When they pass by the beam of light is broken and at that moment their race time is clocked."

"I don't see how it helps us understand why the brothers want Cliff to have slide three." Zack says.

Reese looks more closely at the pictures.

"Battle, look here in the background. What are the brothers doing with the thing they are holding?" Rachel asks.

Reese clicks the mouse to zoom in on what is being held in the picture.

Battle answers, "I see it Rachel. That looks like a speed tracker. We use it in baseball to see how fast a baseball is thrown. I bet the brothers are tracking Cliff to compare his speed to last year."

Rachel talks slow then fast.

"Battle, that could be it, but the slide sensor beam tracks the speed. I think the brothers have a different plan. Bam! I got it!"

Chapter 7

"Rachel, tell us! What are the brothers doing?"
  Battle asks.
  "Don't you see ?
  Rachel looks around at her brothers and sisters
and begins to explain.
  "The brothers are pointing a laser beam *out* of the
tracker. The brothers point the laser bean when
there is no one on the slide."
  "So? I point at my pigs all the time." Zack says.
  Reese continues where Rachel stopped talking.
  "Oh, I get it. If they were going to track Cliff's
speed he would have to be on the slide. He is not
on the slide, but they still point the laser. Why is
37

now the new question."

Battle pushes the screen down to close the laptop computer. Battle jumps up from his seat.

"I got it! They're tricking the sensor to make the judges think Cliff crosses the finish before he actually does. What you have a picture of is the brothers practicing their aim."

Rachel claps with excitement .
"That's it Battle! The laser is what actually crosses the finish line, not the person. This sends the judge's computer a score when the laser crosses the tube slide sensor. The person on the slide does not even have a score recorded! That is why Cliff wants slide number three! I bet the brothers laser has the best angle to slide number three."

With the pieces of the mystery all explained for her Morgan crosses her arms. Morgan is upset.

"Cheaters aren't winners. We have to stop them!"

Reese calls to the front of the RV toward mom.

"Hey mom, were ready to go back to the tubes."

Mom answers with a request to dad.

"Tom, will you take the kids back to the tubes. I'll clean up the RV and meet you there."

"You heard your mom kids. Let's go kids! Back to the waterpark for Moore fun!"

The RV door swings open and one by one the kids exit the RV with dad following behind.

"Kids … wait up, … slow down, what's the rush?"

Dad says to the kids and he walks fast to keep up.

As the family zigs and zags through the parking lot dad calls ahead again.

"I thought we could stop for ice cream. Anyone?"

With no reaction from the kids who are still walking quickly dad does a light jog to keep up.

Dad tries for an answer again.

"Kids, anyone for ice cream?"

Zack does not slow down walking, but answers.

"Dad, you don't understand! We have a mystery!"

Dad smiles.

"Oh Zack, I did not know there was a mystery to solve. Did you solve for the '4M's' yet?"

Zack answers, "I know dad - Motive, Means, Moment and the Moore family. You bet we did! You wouldn't believe it if I told you!"

Dad is now walking next to Zack.

"Wow Zack, you kids sure are busy. I don't want to take away from your plan. I will walk everyone to the tubes and then I will find some ice cream."

Morgan stops walking and looks to dad.

"Now you get it dad! Hey, it's a hot day. How about a piggy-back ride for your youngest?"

"All-abord. Choo-Choo!" Dad cheers.

Morgan is still on dads back as the group get to the *Drain Pipe* tube ride. There is not a single judge or race contestant to be seen.

"Looks like we will have to see Cliff and the judges at the race tomorrow." Rachel says.

Zack turns to ask dad a question.

"Now dad, how about that ice cream?"

Chapter 8

The sun rises at 6:53 am the next day.

The RV lights turn on one at a time as the family wakes up. The kids are excited for the big race and a second day of waterpark rides. The park opens at 8:00 in the morning. The kids want to be the first in the park. The RV rocks and moves as each member of the Moore family hurries to get ready for the day.

After breakfast is over the family exits the RV. It is exactly 7:45 in the morning. The family arrives at the gate just in time for the park opening. The family shows their tickets at the entrance. Zack leads the way. While waving on his family to walk faster Zack sings a song.

"We're gonna solve a mystery.
We will make history.
This is what you're gonna see,
Come on people, follow me!"

Rachel calls to Zack.

"Zack .. Zack .. slow down, wait for us."

Zack stops walking to wait for Rachel. Rachel gets to him and leans down to whisper.

"Psst .. Zack .. don't say or sing anything. We do not want anyone to realize we know their plan. We have to tell the judges first."

"Ah .. got it!" Zack says to Rachel.

"Hey kids .. we have to stop here first. I promised mom to pick up sun lotion in the gift shop."

"Dad, we don't have time. Battle needs to be there in 20 minutes!" Morgan says while tapping her watch with her finger.

"But Morgan, if I look like a daddy tomato with five small tomato's at the end of today mom will be upset. I will need to explain why we each have a sunburn." explains dad

Dad with a wave of his hand signals the kids to

follow him. The family walks to the gift shop.

Inside Reese is bored and questions, "Rachel, why does dad have to read the back of every sun lotion?"

Rachel nods her head up and down.

"I totally agree. Pick up a tube and go, sunblock is sunblock is my vote. But Reese, your saying that about sunblock is funny. You know *I* feel that way about socks, but for you socks are a ten-minute decision in the morning. If you made fashion choices as fast as you make sunblock choices … well, just think of all the time you would have!"

Rachel smiles. Reese is still bored.

A few minutes pass and dad walks to the cash register to pay for the sunblock.

"Battle, hurry and get your brother so we can get you to that race."

"I don't know where he went dad." Battle answers.

Dad uses his thumb to point to the back of the store. Dad tells Battle where to find Zack.

"Zack was over that way trying to balance a stack of hats on his head."

Battle smiles and answers dad.

"I got it dad. One Zack coming right up."

A voice comes on the park speakers.

"Attention 'Drain Pipe' contestants please
line up at the 'Drain Pipe' entry gate.
The race will begin in 5 minutes."

"Guys, we won't have time to talk to the judges! The race is about to start!" Battle says.

Battle continues to talk as he thinks aloud.

"I'll just have to do the race and try to win."

Reese gives her brother a side hug.

"Don't worry Battle, we can tell the judges after the race. You still can win even if Cliff is cheating."

Rachel, Zack and Morgan agree.

"What is this I hear? Someone is not playing fair? Cheating?" asks Dad.

With a pat on dad's back Rachel talks to dad.

"Don't worry dad. I'll fill you in during the race."

Then, as if a big wind pushed the family from the store, Dad, Battle, Rachel, Reese, Morgan and Zack exit the store to go to the *Drain Pipe*.

As the family gets to the *Drain Pipe* ride Morgan stops to wave. With excitement she yells, "Look – there's mom – in the seats by the watching place!"

Mom points to the seats and yells to the family.

"Kids, I am over here! I saved great seats for us all! Reese get your camera ready?"

The family say's good-bye to Battle.

"Go show Cliff how its done Battle!" says Zack.

"You will do great!" Rachel smiles.

"Go Battle!" Morgan cheers.

"I'll take a lot of pictures!" Reese adds.

Then, with a slippery sunblock high-five from dad, and a wave from mom, Battle turns to run to the *Drain Pipe* entry gate.

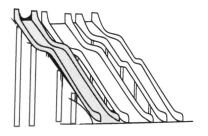

Chapter 9

Twenty minutes pass by on the clock.

"Look! The race is about to start! I see people at the top of each slide." Morgan says as she jumps up from her seat while putting on her big, purple sunglasses.

A bell dings five times to signal a countdown.

Morgan says, "Bam! Here they come!"

Rachel, Reece, Zack, Morgan, mom and dad all clap and cheer for Battle.

"Moore Moore Moore"

The first three racers come out of the tubes. They each splash in the pool at almost the same time. Zack turns to Morgan.

"Aw, man Morgan. That is not Battle. I can't believe I dropped my candy on the floor when I jumped up for nothing. Mom, will you let me know when Battle is really there?"

"Sure Zack. Hey, is now a good time for you? There he is!" mom says with a smile.

The bell begins to ding for a countdown again.

The family begins to cheer and looks with excitement for Battle.

"*Moore Moore Moore*"

"Rachel do you see anything yet?" Reese whispers.

"Not yet .. wait .. wait .. there he is ... see his blue bathing suit! I don't think he is in this group. He is the next race." Rachel says.

"Hey Rachel – see that? The brothers have their secret device pointed at slide three.

Zack overheard and talks loudly for all to hear.

"Cliff must be in this race that is about to start!"

A bell dings five times for a countdown. The racers start and land in the pool under the tubes.

"Wow, that was a close race!" dad says.

Rachel leans into Reese.

"The brothers look very happy. I guess they

47

think they were able to trick the finish times."

"Look, I see Battle!" mom says.

The family stands again.

A bell dings five times to signal a countdown. "*Moore Moore Moore*!"

The family cheers grow louder as Battle slides closer and closer to the pool. Then *splash*! Battle lands in the big pool with a big splash. The family cheers and claps. Battle uses his hand to put a big number one in the air as he smiles.

Reese exclaims, "I can't wait to see the results! It would be great if Battle won the race. That would show the brothers that cheating is not the way."

"Ok kids, two more groups of three will come down the tubes. We will soon hear the winners announced. I am sure Battle will be in the top 12." Dad says.

"Dad, we all know that trick. There are 12 people in the race, so he has to be top 12!" Morgan smiles.

"I'm sure Battle did really well, but no one can beat Cliff. The race is a sham!" Zack says.

"Zack, why do you say no one can beat Cliff? Why is it a sham?" mom questions.

"Mom, you see those two guys over there. We think they are Cliff's brothers. That thing they are holding tricks the finish line. It tricks the finish time so the judges get a different time! That thing the brothers have is why the family wins so much."

"Rachel, Reese, is that true?" The sisters nod their heads up and down to signal yes to their mom.

Mom turns to dad.

"Dad, it looks like you and I should visit the judges table with the kids. We have a story to tell."

Dad agrees.

"Just what I was thinking Maggie. Perhaps we should get an ice cream for the walk?"

Mom laughs as she begins to gather the family's things from the viewing area.

"Ok, ice cream for the walk. Then directly to the judges table." Mom says.

Morgan chimes in with an idea.

"Also we should get one for Battle. He worked hard today!"

Chapter 10

The family enjoys the ice cream while walking to find a judge to hear their story. As mom takes her final ice cream lick she turns to Zack.

"Zack, why are you holding your empty ice cream cone?" mom asks.

"Don't you want to eat the cone?" Dad adds.

Zack smiles and shakes his head.

"Nah, I have a plan."

The family arrives at the judge's table. Zack holds his cone up to his mouth as if it is a microphone.

"Welcome to Moore News. This is Zack Moore talking to you live from the judge's table at *The Bathtub* waterpark."

"Zack, this is hardly the time." Rachel says.

Zack smiles and continues to pretend his cone is a microphone. Zack turns to a pretend T.V. camera and talks again.

"The annual *Drain Pipe* race has just finished. The Moore family is going to tell a judge that there was a cheater in the race."

Zack then holds the cone away from his mouth. Zack points the ice cream come in the direction of dad who is about to talk to a judge.

Mom softly touches Zack's hand.

"Zack, please lower your microphone cone to let your dad talk to the judge."

One of the judges reaches out his hand to dad.

"Hello Sir, my name is Earnest England. I am the park manager. Today I am also a judge. Did you enjoy the race?"

"Actually, I did enjoy the race, but .."

Earnest talks over dad.

"I am glad you are enjoying the park. Do come back next year."

Earnest smiles and turns around to talk the other two judges.

Tapping Earnest on his shoulder dad tries again.

"Earnest, excuse me one more time. My children have something to tell you."

"Yes Sir, your children are welcome next year as well. Thank you for coming."

Earnest is distracted as he is listening to the judge's compute the race score.

Reese takes a few steps over to listen to the judges talk as they review the scores.

"Look at that Nancy, Cliff has done it again!" says judge number three to judge number two.

Hearing this Reese can't control herself.

"No - No, he didn't!"

Earnest finally gives his attention to dad.

Reese has made the comment so loud that everyone in the area heard.

Looking at dad Earnest asks a question.

"Sir, does your daughter have something to say?"

Dad answers with a friendly smile.

"Yes Earnest, she does. Thank you for asking."

Dad looks at Reese and she starts to talk.

"Cliff did not win. Cliff cheated. Well, actually Cliff and his brothers did the cheating!"

Reese looks to Rachel. Rachel talks to the judge.

"Our brother did not have a chance to win!"

Earnest asks Reese and Rachel.

"When someone else wins it can be disappointing. Who is your brother? I am sure he also did well."

Reese answers Earnest the judge with serious tone.

"Battle is our brother, but that is not the problem."

Earnest looks at dad. For a full minute the room is quiet. Zack finds the quiet as his chance to talk.

Zack begins, "Earnest, here is what happened. Cliff has two brothers and –"

Earnest interrupts Zack and stands up tall with a proud smile.

"Yes, each of his brothers has won the *Drain Pipe* race in prior years. A family of champions and they look great on our park posters."

Zack replies, "No, no, no .. a family of cheaters! We have pictures that show the brothers tricking the tube slide to make Cliff win!"

Earnest turns to ask dad, "Is this true?"

"Yes. I am sad to say I saw it myself during the race." Dad answers.

Earnest taps the table to get the attention of the

other two judges.

Looking at Zack, Earnest bends down to talk.

"Young man will you say that again for the other judges to hear."

Zack takes his towel off his shoulder and gives it to mom. Zack holds his ice cream cone to his mouth to "report the news".

"Zack here at the waterpark. Cliff's family is not a family of winners. They are cheaters!"

Rachel looks at the judge's and asks a question.

"Cliff has two brothers. During the race they had a way to trick the sensor at the bottom of the tube. Cliff did not mark his time when the came down the slide. The brothers did with their heat-ray tool!"

Judge number two and judge number three both look at Earnest. They are frozen with open mouths.

Earnest takes a step closer to dad.

"You said that you have pictures to show the brothers with this heat-ray tool?"

Reese steps closer to Earnest and talks.

"Yesterday when Cliff was practicing on the tubes the brothers practiced their aim from the stands. That is when we took some photos. Then today we saw them there again with the heat-ray tool pointing it at slide three during the race. Today the only time they held up the heat-ray was when Cliff came down slide number three."

Dad looked at Earnest. "The kids were able to use the computer to zoom in close on the pictures. The tool said 'Heat-Ray 7000' on the side. I think it was a way to send heat to the slide sensor. You see Earnest, the sensor was tricked to think the heat is a person. The computer records the time as if a person crossed the beam. Since tube three is closest to the viewing stand it is my guess it was the easiest to aim for with the tool."

Mom speaks in a kind, soft tone.

"So you see judges, we don't know which crossed the sensor on tube three first – Cliff or the heat-ray."

Earnest shakes hands with mom and dad. He asks,

"Can you meet me at the Bath Tub office with the pictures in 20 minutes?"

"You bet we will!" Zack answers.

Earnest turns to talk to the judges.

"Looks like we have to find Cliff and his brothers before we announce the winners."

Zack holds the ice cream cone microphone up to his mouth. He turns to his family.

"You heard it here first. The case of the waterpark mystery. Who splashed first ... Cliff or one of the other people in the race? Join us at the *Bath Tub* office in 20 minutes for more."

Chapter 11

"Look! That must be the waterpark office mom. I see the sign, 'Bath Tub Security.'" Reese says.

Zack is excited and speaks loudly.

"Time to show some pictures to the judges!"

Dad holds the big blue door open. The family enters the security office.

Inside the family is welcomed by the three judges.

"Have a seat. We are just waiting on Cliff and his brothers." Smiles judge number two.

The security office is filled with sunshine. You can see a waterpark ride from every one of the seven windows. The seats are all different colors. Zack and Morgan are excited to pick a chair color. The door opens slowly. Cliff and his two brothers enter the room. The brothers choose each choose to sit in a red chair. Cliff chooses a yellow chair.

Earnest the judge starts to talk.

"Looks like we can begin. Mr. and Mrs. Moore, will you please tell the group your concern?"

Mom answers Earnest.

"Thank you Earnest. My children saw two people. I think they are brothers. They had a tool that appeared to help their brother Cliff win the race."

Battle stands from his chair.

"I did see the pictures. My brother Zack heard the brothers say they wanted to be sure Cliff was on slide number three."

Rachel interrupts, ".. and here are the pictures."

Rachel opens her laptop and puts it on the desk. She open the computer to show them the pictures.

Cliff stands up fast from his chair.

"Judges, they are wrong. I did not cheat!"

One of the brothers touches Cliff on his arm.

The brother asks, "Cliff, sit down? Please."

Cliff looks at his brother with a confused face. Cliff then sits down and moves his ams and hands to ask his brothers. Cliff does not know why his brother asked him to sit down.

The room is quiet.

The judges whisper softly as they review the pictures on the computer. The judges also look at the race time results. They whisper and point and point and whisper. The words of each judge are not loud enough for anyone in the Moore family to hear.

The Moore family can only sit and wait for a judge to talk.

Cliff and his brothers also wait.

The room is quiet.

After four minutes the silence is broken when one of Cliff's brothers stands up and talks.

"Cliff did not do anything wrong!"

Earnest is surprised.

"Do you have something to add? Do keep talking. Did you have some facts of your own here?"

The brother looks down at the floor and talks.

"Yes sir. My brother and I were wrong. Our idea was to help Cliff; he always comes in third behind us. It has been hard on him. We thought after seeing how proud he was last year from his win that we would help him win again this year. We did not think that helping Cliff would matter to the other people in race."

Cliffs stands up and is mad.

He looks at his brothers. He looks at Battle. Then he turns and quickly exits the room. The big blue door closes with a bang.

Morgan stands up and points at the brothers.

"Look what you did! Because of you my brother was not in a fair race! You guys better be sorry to my brother – and your brother!"

Dad signals Morgan to sit back down in her chair.

Earnest looks at mom and dad, he stands to talk.

"The judges have made a decision about what to do with the race results. We will cross the time results with the waterpark video of the event. Then we will compare the results to the pictures taken by your family. If it appears the brothers altered Cliff's score then Cliff will be removed from the contestant list."

Rachel stands up along with her family as they prepare to leave. Rachel looks at Earnest and talks.

"Thank you Earnest for listening to our concerns."
Earnest walks to the blue door and holds it open
for the family.

"Thank you Moore family for coming forward
with your pictures. We pride ourselves on a fair
race. So y'all can leave now and take a seat in the
award area by the slides. You will hear the winners
names in one hour." Earnest says.

The Moore family leaves the security office. The
family rests at a bench close by in the shade.

"Great job kids. You solved the mystery using
the '4M's!" Dad says with a smile.

"Oh dad, not again!" Reese laughs.

"It's ok Reese, let your dad have his moment."
says mom.

"I have a question for you kids. For one
super-puffy, pink cotton candy, who remembers
the "4M'"s?" Dad says while pointing at his head.

Battle answers first.

"You bet dad. The first is *means*. Did the brothers
have *a means* (a way) to change the results? The
answer is … yes, they did. They were in the park
and had the 'Heat-Ray.'"

Rachel continues, "Next is *motive*; the reason for cheating. The brothers said themselves their motive was they wanted Cliff to win and feel proud. So that would be their motive."

Zack gloats, "Moment is third; and they were there alright. I saw them on the bleachers myself! I saw the moment! Without me Cliff would be getting those $100 Bathtub Bucks prize for sure! "

Morgan finishes with the forth M.

"Moore is the last M; our family is the best!"

Dad gives each of the kids a high-five. Then he stands with his arms crossed and looks at mom.

"Look at that Maggie. Our kids *do* listen to me! Follow me everyone! It is cotton candy time!"

Chapter 12

The park speaker turns on and words begin to come out for everyone to hear.

"Attention park guests. The awards for 'The Drain Pipe' race will be given in 5 minutes."

"Let's go Moore family! We have a brother who needs a medal!" raves Zack.

"Zack, we don't even know if I won, but I am happy to hear you have faith in me," answers Battle.

The family picks up their sunscreen and towels. They leave behind a trash pail with seven empty cotton candy sticks as they walk to the event.

"Whew, we are here just in time!" says Reese. Earnest is on small stand talking into a microphone.

"The results have been decided. Thank y'all for showin' up today."

The crowd claps and Earnest talks again.

"Each of the first, second and third place winners will get a medal and 'Bath Tub bucks'. The 'Bath Tub bucks' are for the gift store right here at the front of the park. For all you non-winners, cash and card will also do just fine. Now, back to the winners. "

The crowd claps and cheers.

"Now the winners. In third place we have Eddie Lewis from Alabama."

Eddie runs to the stage with his arms in the air. Eddie places his medal on his neck and holds 25 Bath Tub bucks in the air.

Earnest continues.

"In second place we have Battle Moore from Tennessee. Battle, please come up for your medal and 50 'Bath Tub bucks.'"

Zack cheers and squeals like a pig as the family claps. Battle walks to the stage and gets his second place medal and "Bathtub Bucks" Battle stops walking so he can pose as Reese takes a picture.

Rachel leans over and whispers to Reese.

"Do you think that means Cliff won first place?"

Reese thinks about the question and whispers.

"With my photos there is no way the judges could have ignored the proof. I am sure of it."

Earnest continues to announce the awards from the stage.

"In first place, we are proud to award a medal plus 100 'Bath Tub bucks'. The winner, , with a time of 42.8 seconds, is Miss Olivia-Bella Odin from Georgia." The crowd cheers and watches as Olivia jumps up and down.

"Olivia, please come to the stage." Earnest asks.

Olivia continues to celebrate with her family.

"Olivia, are you coming? We want to ensure everyone has a chance to visit the gift shop. Ah, ok folks, here she comes."

Earnest claps and Olivia comes to the stage.

Morgan tugs on Resse's shirt to ask a question.

"Um .. guys .. isn't that Cliff coming this way?"

"Yep, sure is." Zack groans.

"Its ok guys. I got this." Battle says.

Cliff arrives at the group and looks at Battle.

"Battle, I am here because I feel so sad about the

race. I am sorry. I did not know my brothers had a plan. I would have liked to compete against you on my own. They took that chance away from me. I hope you can forgive me."

Cliff looks hopeful and talks again.

"I am glad you won a medal."

Battle looks at his family and answers Cliff.

"Cliff, you are a good contestant. I am glad to have met you. It was not right to rig the race, but they did it because they want the best for you. I hope you sign up again next year." Battle says.

"Battle, you are on! I hope to see you at the race next year."

Cliff raises his hand and receives a high five from Battle. As Cliff walks away he stops to look back and wave good-bye to the family.

Mom picks up Morgan and asks a question.

"Moore family, who is ready for morrrre pool time?"

The sun begins to go down. The day park guests begin to leave. After a long and wet day at the waterpark the family returns to the RV.

The family puts on dry clothes and gets set in their seats. Over the voices mom lets dad know its is time to go.

"Ok dad, time to hit the road! Next stop ... Orlando, Florida!"

Reese is excited and cheers.

"Yes! I am ready for the sunshine and fun rides!"

Rachel answers her.

"You bet! The sun, the rides and I can't wait to read about local history."

Morgan teases Zack.

"Hey Zack, maybe we will see a pig farm!"

"Aw, now I miss Hazel. Why did you have to say that? Mom, can Farmer Hammond send me a picture of my pigs?" Zack asks.

"I will ask Farmer Hammond for a picture when I talk with him Zack. For now, let us get comfortable for our drive," says mom.

Zack whispers to mom.

"Mom, can you give us a hint about the next family-fun-stop? Where are we going?"

Mom turns to Zack and talks loud enough for all to hear her answer.

"Our next adventure will be with my friend and her children. What we will do there is a surprise."

Dad begins, "Buckle up kids –" but is stopped by the family who talk at the same time.

"…For Moooore safety."
Dad nods his head
"Sit back and enjoy the drive."

The RV horn hunks seven times and the family drives south to the next family-fun-stop.

Splash!

Workbook Pages
Quiz

Vocabulary Words
Study the list below.

1. ADVENTURE – A FUN TRIP OR VACATION

2. REALIZE – TO LEARN SOMETHING

3. CHAMPION – THE WINNER

4. CONTESTANT – A PLAYER IN A GAME

5. MYSTERY – SOMETHING NOT KNOWN

6. PRACTICE – TO TRY, TO GET BETTER

7. UPLOAD – TO PUT ONTO A COMPUTER

8. REQUIRE – SOMETHING NEEDED

9. PERMANENT – FOREVER, NOT LIKELY TO CHANGE

10. INSTRUCT – TO TEACH OR SHOW

11. DEVICE – A TOOL USED TO DO A TASK

12. ANNOUNCE – TO SAY SOMETHING LOUDLY

13. INTERRUPT – TO TALK OVER SOMEONE

14. CONFESS – TO TELL THE TRUTH

15. COMPETE – TO PLAY IN A GAME

Vocabulary Practice

Choose the synonym for each word.
A synonym is two words that are different, but have the same meaning.

1. ADVENTURE: **bedtime**   **vacation**   **cleaning**

2. REALIZE: **learn**   **feel**   **touch**

3. CHAMPION: **winner**   **player**   **teacher**

4. CONTESTANT: **friend**   **sport**   **player**

5. MYSTERY: **unknown**   **birthday**   **rainbow**

6. PRACTICE: **to read**   **to watch**   **to try**

7. UPLOAD: *TO PUT ON A*: **wall**   **computer**   **table**

8. REQUIRE: **need**   **want**   **see**

9. PERMANENT: **one time**   **forever**   **never**

10. INSTRUCT: **learn**   **read**   **teach**

11. DEVICE: **a food**   **a tool**   **a movie**

12. ANNOUNCE: **to say**   **to read**   **to do**

13. INTERRUPT: *TO TALK*:   **after**   **during**   **before**

14. CONFESS: **say the truth**   **say a lie**   **be quiet**

15. COMPETE: **to go agsinst**   **to read**   **to write**

STUDY THE LIST BELOW.

1. always
2. children
3. contestants
4. excitement
5. family
6. Georgia
7. impossible
8. medal
9. mystery
10. pencil
11. picture
12. practice
13. shoulder
14. tomorrow
15. whisper

Spelling Practice

Circle the word that is spelt correctly.

1. ALLWAYS ALWAYSE ALWAYS

2. CHILDREN CHILREN CHILLDREN

3. CONTESTENTS CONTESTANTS CANTESTANTS

4. EXCITEMENT EXCITEMENT EXCITEMINT

5. FAMILY FAMELY FAMEILY

6. GORGIA GEORGIA GEORGEA

7. IMPOSSIBLE IMPOSSIBLY IMPOSSIBLEE

8. MADAL METALE MEDAL

9. MISTERY MESTERY MYSTERY

10. PENCIL PENNSIL PENSIL

11. PICTARE PICHURE PICTURE

12. PRECTACE PRACTYCE PRACTICE

13. SHOULDER SHOWLDER SHOLDER

14. TAMOROW TOMORROW TOMOROW

15. WHIZPER WHISPPER WHISPER

So Many Ways To Say 'Say'

Imagine you are writing a book.
Draw a line to match the word on the left
with the feeling of the speaker on the right.

Admits	Happy
Apologizes	Confused
Cheers	Scared
Laughs	Guilty
Orders	Quiet
Questions	Sorry
Screams	Hopeful
Whispers	Bossy

Search the Book

Search the book to find the answer.

1. Who are the Moore children?
The oldest child in the family is _____.
The twins are _____ and _____.
The next child is _____.
The youngest child is _____.

2. The family farm is located in _____.

3. The tool the brothers used was _____.

4. The name of one judge was _____.

5. There were _____ winners in the race.

6. The four M's to solve a mystery are:
1. _____ 2. _____
3. _____ 4. _____

7. Battle won a _____ and _____.

this page intensionally left blank

End of Book Quiz   Score: _____/_ 18_

Circle T if the sentence is true, F if it is false.

1. T F   Rachel is the oldest child.
2. T F   The family travels in a van.
3. T F   Zack adores his pigs.
4. T F   Reese likes to take pictures.
5. T F   Dad enjoys ice cream.
6. T F   The ride is called the Great Tube.
7. T F   The race has three slides.
8. T F   Battle does not practice for the race.
9. T F   Morgan overhears the brothers plan.
10. T F   The brothers want Cliff on slide two.
11. T F   Zack uploads pictures to a computer.
12. T F   Cliff's brothers attend the race.
13. T F   Battle is the second place winner.
14. T F   The third place winner is from Ohio.
15. T F   Cliff is on the poster in the park.
16. T F   Rachel wants to go to Florida.
17. T F   The family will be staying in a hotel.
18. T F   The family is now driving to Texas.

Morgan and Zack see Farmer Hammond.

Our Bags Are Ready To Go!

Answer Key

P. 73   Vocabulary Practice

1. vacation 2. learn 3. winner 4. player
5. unknown 6 to try 7. to put on a computer
8. need 9. forever 10. teach 11. a tool
12. to say 13. to talk during
14. say the truth 15. to go against

P. 75   Spelling Practice

Please see the spelling word list on page 74.

P. 76   Ways to say say

Admits:Guilty   Apologizes:Sorry

Cheers:Happy   Laughs:Happy

Orders:Bossy   Questions:Confused

Screams:Scared   Whispers:Quiet

P. 77   Search The Book

1. Battle, Rachel and Reese, Zack, Morgan
2. Tennessee   3. Heat-Ray 4. Earnest
5. Three 6. Means, motive, moment, Moore.
7. A 2nd place medal and $50 Bathtub Bucks

Quiz Answer Key

Circle T if the sentence is true, F if it is false.

1. T **F**   *Battle* is the oldest child.
2. T **F**   The family travels in **An RV**
3. **T** F   Zack adores his pigs.
4. **T** F   Reese likes to take pictures.
5. **T** F   Dad enjoys ice cream.
6. T **F**   The ride is called **The Drain Pipe**
7. **T** F   The race has three slides.
8. T **F**   Battle do **Does** t practice for the race.
9. T **F**   M **Zack** n overhears the brothers plan.
10. T **F**   The brothers want Cliff on slide **Three**
11. T **F**   **Reese** uploads pictures to a computer.
12. **T** F   Cliff's brothers attend the race.
13. **T** F   Battle is the second place winner.
14. T **F**   The third place winner is from **Georgia**
15. **T** F   Cliff is on the poster in the park.
16. **T** F   Rachel wants to go to Florida.
17. T **F**   The family will be staying in an **An RV**.
18. T **F**   The family is now driving to **Florida**

82

Hi!
Thanks for reading about
the adventure my
family and I had in Georgia.
Join us on our next stop, Florida!
See you soon!
Reese

Dad's Favorite

Our Discovery

HEATRAY 7000-4

Battle practices for the race.

Rachel shows Battle the Drain Pipe.

**Engaging and Fun
plus
Skill Builders & a Book Quiz
in the back of every
YMBA learning book.**

**An easy way to demonstrate
learning accomplishments.**

We know our children read books,
but do they read to retain?
How do we demonstrate reading completion?
The end of book quiz is a great idea!

Have you read 57 Days?

A fictional adventure based on factual events.

Join Miriam, Adam and Anne Mary, on their journey from England to America with William Penn to see the land he was granted in the New World by the King of England. Exciting history based on actual people and events. Experience the triumphs, struggles, loss and dreams while traveling across the Atlantic Ocean to a new home. Discover the path so many experienced as they left their home for America. Details vividly paint a picture of the conditions on the ship and the difficult days along the way. What challenges did they endure? What were the fears and hopes of the young adults? An exciting historical adventure of the journey to America. Join Miriam on her voyage with her family and William Penn.

GRADES 6-10/AGES 11-15/ FACTION CHAPTER BOOK

Y.M.B.A. Teen Business

Y.M.B.A. learning workbooks are designed with students 12 to 16 in mind.

THINK

STRATEGIZE

INVESTIGATE

APPLY

CREATE

COMPUTE

EXPLORE

- Lessons that teach on the left and worksheets on the right
- Practical examples that encourage strategic thinking
- Effectively practice topic skills considering real-world ideas
- Expand business vocabulary skills and explore strategic creativity
- Complete an end of book quiz to demonstrate learning success

2018 AMAZON PRICE PROMO for a limited time

Business Skills

Book Quiz Included

Life Skills

Search "YMBA Business" at www.Amazon.com

Coming Soon!
Consumer Math
Business Math II
Management
Sports Marketing

Learning workbooks may be enjoyed in any sequence.